THE BIG PARADE

Story by
Karen M. Hefty

Programmed by
John Hefty

Illustrations by Valarie Webb

Special Thanks to Wanda Baker & Karen Meissner

Copyright© 1988   Create-A-Book, Inc.   Milton, Florida
Printed in USA

2

This book was created

especially for

Katie Howington

With Love From

Sheryl Sugerman

December 25, 1988

Katie Howington, age 2, sat up wide awake in her bed. The sun was just coming up in Gainesville, Florida. She could tell that it was going to be a gorgeous day. When she glanced out her bedroom window, Katie remembered exactly where she was planning to go today with Mommy, Daddy and Uncle Kendall.

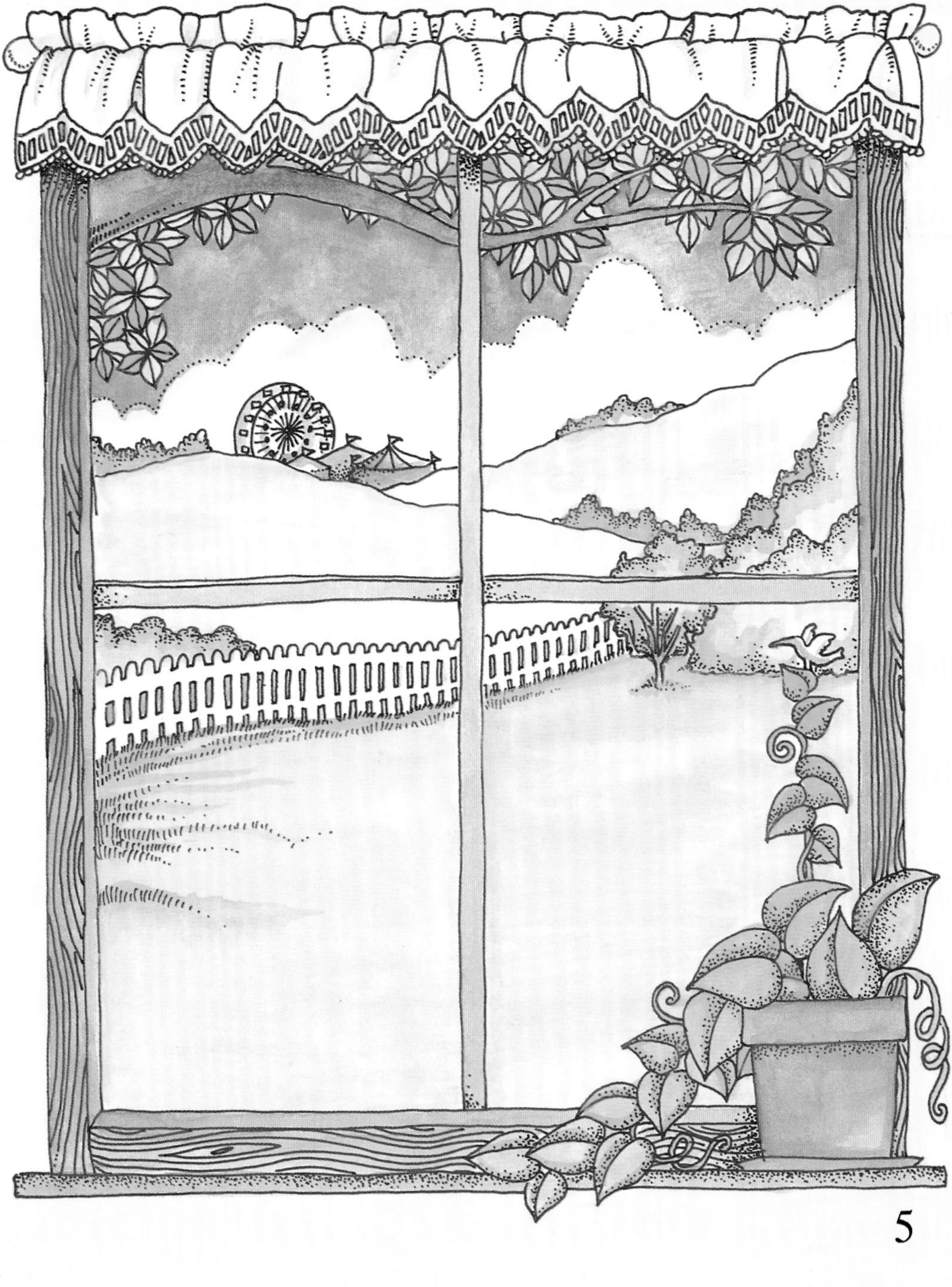

6

Katie had been so excited for the past week. With Mommy, Daddy and Uncle Kendall, she had made a game of finding the most circus posters all over town. Today was the big parade and that meant the start of all the circus activities. Katie had even tried to go to sleep as fast as she could last night to make the morning come more quickly.

Katie began to think about all the

fantastic fun she would have. Last year,

her favorite act was the clown with the

invisible dog. Katie wondered if he would

be there again today. Then she thought

about the child who would be selected

this year by the mayor to lead the parade.

Who would that lucky person be?

9

Just then the phone rang. "Katie Howington, will you lead the big parade for us this year?" asked the mayor of Gainesville, Florida. "Oh, yes, yes!" exclaimed Katie. "Will I get to ride in the fire truck?" The mayor chuckled, "You most certainly will, Katie!"

Mommy, Daddy and Uncle Kendall were waiting with Katie when a huge helicopter landed in her back yard. It was there to pick up Katie. The helicopter took off minutes later with Katie in the front seat grinning from ear to ear. After waving goodbye, Mommy, Daddy and Uncle Kendall hurried downtown, so they would not be late for the parade.

13

From the helicopter, Katie could see the circus parade beginning to assemble at the edge of town. The helicopter landed and Katie ran to the mayor. On their way to the shiny, red fire truck at the head of the parade, they walked past all the practicing performers and anxious animals that would be following Katie.

Someone shouted, "Look, Katie Howington is leading the parade this year!" At that very moment, a big drum roll was heard. Katie carefully climbed aboard the fire truck next to the driver who was dressed like a clown. Katie enjoyed the marvelous, marching music played by the band as the fire truck drove down the main street of Gainesville, Florida.

Immediately behind the band was a beautiful bareback rider. Her two magnificent, prancing horses were so well trained that the rider could balance on both their backs while standing up. Katie imagined that the fine, fancy feathers on the noble horses' heads were bobbing to the beat of the music.

When the fire truck turned a corner, Katie saw three small children mimicking the dancing bear who was dressed in a pink ballerina costume. The big, brown bear was very entertaining as she proudly performed bouncy, ballet steps while balancing on a ball.

21

The circus elephants followed next. As she watched the playful pranks of the darling baby elephant, Katie daydreamed about taking him home. When the elephant fanned his big, floppy ears, Katie could almost picture him flying through the sky with the greatest of ease. If the baby strayed too far, the mother would lovingly wrap her trunk around his.

A jolly juggler on a unicycle juggling five full bottles fascinated Mommy, Daddy and Uncle Kendall. He pedaled so fast that there were times when it was hard for them to keep up with him. They thought it was incredible that he never dropped a bottle, no matter how fast he pedaled. They knew it took practice to be that good.

Katie was amused by the antics of the slippery seal. The seal would flip the ball backwards and then, with his hind flippers, smack it right back to the tip of his nose. Everyone loved watching the seal clap after each trick he performed. Mommy, Daddy and Uncle Kendall had fun imitating his funny, barking noises.

The acrobatic troupe was next. Their tumbling and flipping routines had the crowd cheering. Katie was enjoying her place of honor, but was really tickled when the driver told her she would have a chance to watch the entire parade pass before her as each act entered the big top circus tent.

A majestic lion with all his marvelous mane was in the last wagon. He was so-o-o big, and his roar was so-o-o loud that Katie could hear him from the very front of the parade. The mild-mannered monkeys on top of his cage did not seem at all frightened of the ferocious feline.

The fire truck stopped at the entrance of the big top circus tent. Katie talked to each of the circus stars as they went inside. It made her feel like an important star also to be so close to them. Then Katie joined Mommy, Daddy and Uncle Kendall in her special section inside the tent.

34

When the circus was over, Katie was escorted outside by the mayor and the ringmaster. Katie did not want this special day to end. As she turned to look one last time, some performers were waving goodbye. Katie waved back and smiled, for she knew she would never forget the day she led the big parade!

Katie Howington

Enjoy this special gift from

Sheryl Sugerman

December 25, 1988